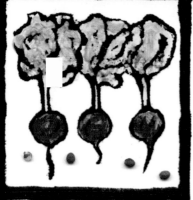

PLANT A LITTLE SEED

Bonnie Christensen

A NEAL PORTER BOOK
ROARING BROOK PRESS
NEW YORK

Copyright © 2012 by Bonnie Christensen

A Neal Porter Book

Published by Roaring Brook Press

Roaring Brook Press is a division of Holtzbrinck Publishing Holdings Limited Partnership

175 Fifth Avenue, New York, New York 10010

mackids.com

Library of Congress Cataloging-in-Publication Data

Christensen, Bonnie.

Plant a little seed / Bonnie Christensen.

p. cm.

"A Neal Porter Book."

Summary: Two friends plant seeds in their community garden, then water, weed, wait, and dream as the plants grow until they can be harvested. Includes facts about gardening and harvest festivals.

ISBN 978-1-59643-550-6

[1. Gardening—Fiction.] I. Title.

PZ7.C45235Pl 2012

[E]—dc22

2011005202

Roaring Brook Press books are available for special promotions and premiums. For details contact: Director of Special Markets, Holtzbrinck Publishers.

First edition 2012

Book design by Jennifer Browne

Printed in December 2011 in China by Macmillan Production Asia Ltd.,

Dongguan City, Guangdong Province (supplier code 10)

1 3 5 7 9 8 6 4 2

To James and Sherman, whose friendship
was the best thing to grow in any garden.
With special thanks to Jacob, Charlene and Ashley Dienes,
Jamie Gross, and Ella Pearsall! —B.C.

We plant a little seed or two
or three or four or more,
then pat the soil, warm in the sun,

and water and wait

and wait and dream . . .

. . . and dream and
wait some more.

One day, at last! A tiny sprout,
then two, then three; then four,
with stems unbending toward the sun
and small leaves stretching skyward.

Greening, growing up and out,

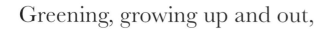

spreading roots way down below.
We water and weed
and dream and wait
and dream and wait some more.

some grow down,

Some plants grow up,

some grow fast,

some grow slowly.

TOMATO

Until, surprise! A yellow bud,
a white bud too, grow to bursting
in the sun.

First the bud, then the flower,
then the flower droops and falls,
soon the fruit begins to grow.

PEA

Our garden sings with buzzing bees,
with rustling leaves and cawing crows,
with gentle rain and whirring wings.

We water and weed
and dream and wait
and water and wait some more.

When the fruit's the perfect size
we munch it warm right off the vine,

sweet and sharp upon our tongues,
we hold the taste of summertime.

Days and weeks and months pass by.
The moon grows huge and bright and gold,
crickets chirp and geese honk high.
All are singing "harvest time."

We gather in our garden's gifts
to pickle, bake, or freeze, or dry,
then cook a glorious autumn
feast—soups and salads,
cakes and pies.

We boil or bake or simmer slow.
I wipe my hands and close my eyes,
inhale the garden's rhapsody.
We cook and wait until it's time

to gather those we love the most,
then pile the harvest table high,
and sing a song of gratitude
for seeds and soil, rain and sun,
and all the springtimes yet to come,
when we . . .

. . . plant a little seed or two.

COMMUNITY
GARDEN NEWS

Seeds come from flowers and fruits. Some seeds look familiar, like peas, corn kernels, and beans. The seeds of some plants are harder to identify, like beets, carrots, broccoli, and radishes.

Seeds need water (but not too much) and warmth to sprout.

Sprouts need water, warmth, and light to grow.

Seed packets tell when to plant, how much space a plant needs, and how long it will take to produce fruits or vegetables. If you start growing your plants indoors, you'll give them a head start.

Some plants, like nasturtiums, grow quickly.

Some plants, like watermelons, take longer to produce fruits or vegetables.

A vegetable is a part of the plant that does not contain seeds. So a vegetable is the flower (broccoli), stem (celery), leaf (lettuce), or root (carrot) of the plant.

A fruit is a part of the plant that contains seeds, like apples and oranges. Tomatoes, zucchini, and peas, which we tend to think of as vegetables, are actually fruits.

Many plants need insects, particularly bees to pollinate flowers so fruits and vegetables will grow. Gardens need worms to keep the soil soft and ladybugs, dragonflies, and spiders to eat garden pests.

Harvest festivals have been celebrated for thousands of years by many different cultures around the world. In the United States and Canada we celebrate Thanksgiving.